D1519055

Mario hopped out of bed, ran downstairs, and plopped down in front of a fruit bowl and a stack of pancakes.

"Good morning, dad!"

"Good morning, Mario. Today is the day we go to the history museum."

"I know, I know!" Mario sang as he spun around in a big circle.

Mario's dad laughed at his excitement.

"Sit down and eat your breakfast, Mario. You'll need all of your energy. Museums are full of things to see."

Written By Rebecca Dupas, Ph.D.
Illustrated by C.J. Love

Merry Christmas '20
from Michel

I'm excited for you to meet Mario!
[signature]

Copyright © 2020 by Rebecca Dupas

Illustrations copyright © 2020 by C.J. Love

All rights reserved. No part of this publication may be reproduced, or transmitted in any form or by any means, including photocopying, recording, or other electronic or mechanical methods, without the prior written permission of the publisher.

Published by: Rebecca Dupas
Printed in the United States of America

In the car, Mario looked at the tall city buildings.

"Dad, what are museums like?"

"Museums are where we can explore new things. They can be fun, but they also hold precious items."

"Precious items like Grandma's favorite dishes?" Mario asked.

"Exactly. Those dishes can't be replaced, so Grandma does her best to keep them safe." Mario smiled because he understood.

"This museum is special because it teaches about us", his dad continued.

"Am I in the museum, dad?" Mario asked with raised eyebrows.

"In a way, yes!" His dad replied. Mario was confused.

"You'll see, son! You'll see."

After he parked the car, Mario's dad grabbed his hand.
"This way," he exclaimed as they walked eagerly through the huge front doors.

HALL OF KINGS ←

THE APACHE

Mario looked around the large, museum lobby. There were high ceilings and hallways leading to rooms he could explore. He ran ahead.

"Wait, son! Museums hold precious items. No running."

"OK," Mario said with his head low. "I thought that museums are places I can explore."

"They are! But they also have rules, just like libraries and schools. Besides, you're my precious item. I have to keep you safe, too."

MUSEUM RULES

🏃 No running

🥤 No food

👆 Do not touch the art

Mario walked swiftly with his dad into the Hall of Kings. "Wow! Do you see that, dad?" Mario exclaimed.

Right before Mario was a tall statue of an Egyptian pharaoh. "Whoa! Who is that?" He asked.

"That's Ramses the Great. He was a great warrior who brought prosperity and stability to Egypt."

"Black men were kings?" Mario asked in wonder.

"Yes. Black women were queens, too!" Mario's father said matter-of-factly. Mario smiled and skipped along.

Mario saw large portraits of men and women in villages. Some were dressed in bright, colorful clothing. Others were wearing only small coverings on their body. Mario's eyes grew big at their body paint and tribal fabrics. "African people are very diverse. They are amazing and powerful people," his dad said.

"Mmmmm Hmmmmm!" Mario shook his head in agreement.

MAP
OF
AFRICA

SOUTH
ATLANTIC
OCEAN

Mario moved close to a large, clay mask. A loud buzz interrupted the silence. Mario jumped as people in the gallery turned to look at him. He was embarrassed and scared. His dad stooped down to comfort him.

DO NOT TOUCH
MUSEUM
ARTIFACTS.

"It's OK, son. That's just a reminder not to get too close. This precious item is breakable. Remembering not to touch it is our way of making sure that other people can learn about it too."

In the next room, Mario saw TV screens and puzzles on the walls. "Go on, son," his dad said encouragingly.

"But I thought you said museums hold precious items and that we couldn't get close?" Mario's dad explained, "Some places in museums require us to explore only with our minds, and other places give us permission to explore with our hands. The more we visit museums, the easier it will be for you to figure when to touch and when to look.

Mario decided to touch colorful buttons and different animal skins. He even watched a cartoon with a little boy in Africa who looked just like him.

PUZZLES

Mario's curiosity led him to visit other places in the museum too. They walked past animals that looked real but didn't move, jewelry that looked too heavy to wear, cool gadgets, and other inventions. Mario had never seen anything like it.

At the end of the big hallway, Mario and his dad stopped and peered into a dark room. Mario's dad put his arm around him.

"This room shows our people being mistreated. We don't have to have this discussion, today. We can always come back."

Mario saw the word "Slavery" on the wall ahead.

"No, dad. I want to learn," Mario said in a low voice. "I've heard that word before."

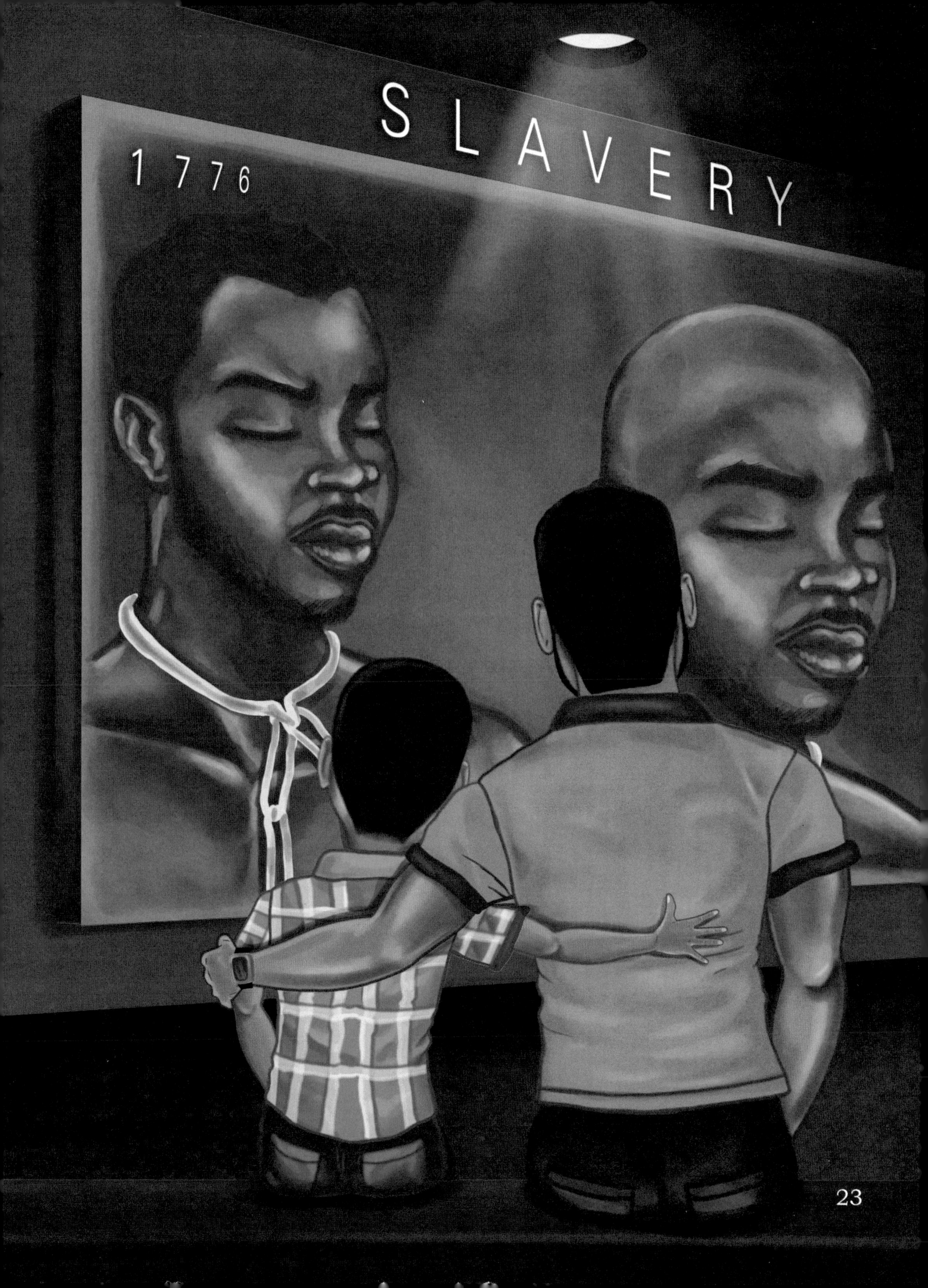
SLAVERY
1776

Mario stared at a large drawing of a slave ship.

"Why would anyone do this, dad?"

"American settlers took Africans to the Americas to unfairly work for free for hundreds of years, son. It's an upsetting and complicated story that we can take our time to understand."

"Is slavery over?" Mario asked.

"This kind of slavery ended a long time ago. You and I are our ancestors' wildest dreams! We are living the kind of life they fought for. Still, I am doing everything I can to make sure you feel free everyday. One day, you will do the same for your children."

Mario smiled as they walked out of the last room.

25

Back in the lobby, Mario looked around at all the people. A little girl ran across the lobby. A baby cried in the distance. In the corner, a group of teenagers talked energetically. "Uh oh," Mario exclaimed when the little girl ran into a man in a uniform.

The security guard told her "No running!" in a big voice and the little girl cried. Mario was glad that his dad explained museums to him. He hoped that the little girl's parents would remind her that she was a precious item too.

MUSEUM
LOBBY

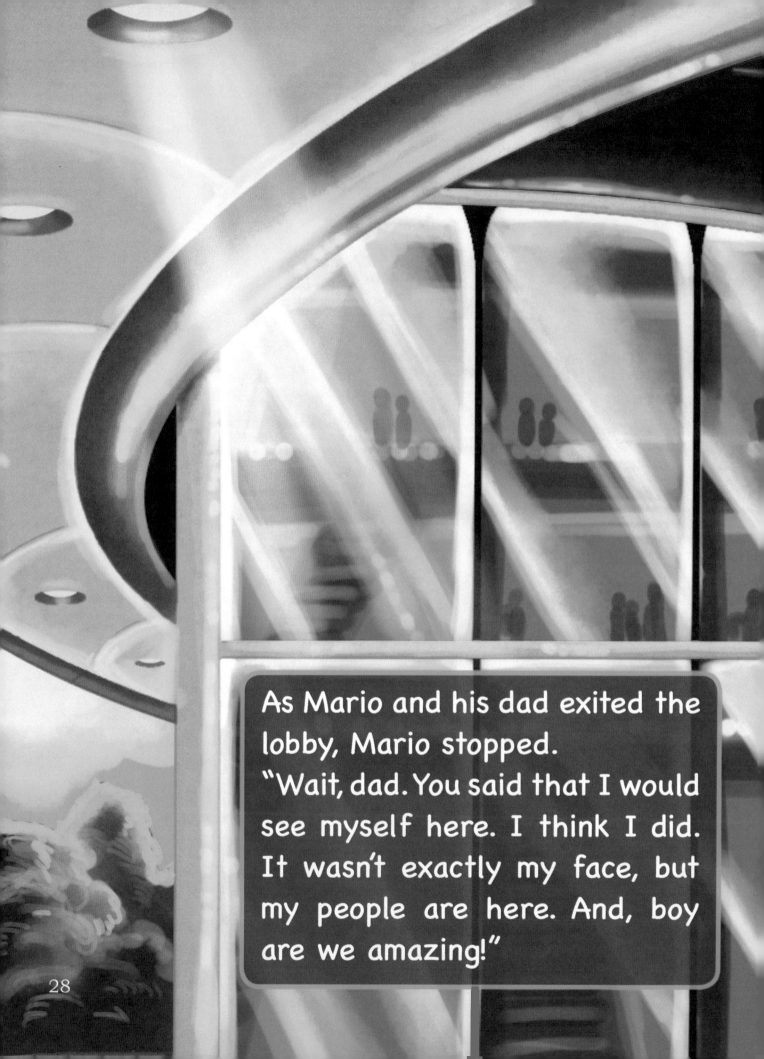

As Mario and his dad exited the lobby, Mario stopped.
"Wait, dad. You said that I would see myself here. I think I did. It wasn't exactly my face, but my people are here. And, boy are we amazing!"

"Mario Goes to the Museum"
Question Guide

Comprehension Questions for All Children:

1. What did you like most about the museum Mario visited?
2. Have you ever been to a museum before? Describe your trip.
3. When is Mario the most excited in the book? Why?
4. When is Mario nervous or upset? Why?
5. How did Mario's dad help him in the museum?
6. Name all the "precious items" in the story. Who are they important to?
7. What museum rules did Mario learn?
8. What did Mario learn about Africa while at the museum?
9. What did Mario learn about himself while at the museum?
10. If you could ask Mario any question, what would it be?

Additional Discussion Questions for Older Children:

1. This was Mario's first time going to a museum. If you had a choice of which museum you could make your first visit to, what museum or what topic would you explore?
2. Why are museums important to different communities of people?
3. Why do you think it's so important to not touch "precious items" in museums?
4. What do you think was Mario's favorite place in the museum. Why?
5. What actions did the museum security guard take in the story? How do you think Mario feels about the guard?
6. Can you think of three ways that museum guards keep us and museums safe?
7. What did Mario's dad mean when he told Mario that he was a "precious item" too?
8. What was the difference between the items that Mario could touch and the items he couldn't touch in the museum?
9. Think back to where you see Mario and his dad hug. Why do you think they needed to hug in those moments? What can hugs symbolize?
10. What precious item in your home would you like to put in a museum so that people could learn about its importance forever?
11. If you could build a museum and include five things that would tell people more about you or your culture, what would you include?
12. Can you name three types of museum jobs? What skills would a person need to be successful at each job?
13. Look back at the pictures in the book. What additional information can we assume about Mario and the museum from the book illustrations?

About the Author

Dr. Rebecca Dupas is a photographer, award-winning poet, and author whose work has appeared on Fox 5, C- Span, PBS News, and in The Washington Post. "Mario Goes to the Museum" emerges as a perfect blend of her many passions. His fictional experience pulls from her role as a former classroom teacher, museum educator, and researcher of diversity training and education. Connect and read more at **rebeccadupas.com**.

About the Illustrator

C. J. Love is a graduate of the Maryland Institute College of Art with a Bachelor of Fine Arts degree in Graphic Design. He specializes in illustration, caricatures, mural painting, graphic design, and prototype designs. Visit at **www.clove2design.com**

Made in the USA
Middletown, DE
01 December 2020

24940723R00020